CHAPTER 1

"Jeepers, this dance club is cool," I said as the gang and I walked into the DanceKraze club. Colorful lights flashed all around us. The beat of loud rock music pounded.

"You'd better hurry, Shaggy," Fred said. "You don't want to be late for your DJ tryout."

"Like, don't call me Shaggy," Shaggy said. "My DJ name is Baggy. It goes with my baggy pants, part of my happening look."

"Rat's right," Scooby agreed.

"And don't call him Scooby," Shaggy continued. "His DJ name is Scoob-Doggy-Dogg."

"Wow!" Daphne said with a laugh. "You guys are cutting-edge!"

"Absolutely," Shaggy — I mean "Baggy" — agreed. "Speaking of cutting-edge, I wonder if someone could cut us some ham and cheese for a sandwich. I'm starved."

"How unusual," I joked. When wasn't Shaggy starved? Even his tryout for a DJ job in a dance club didn't make him nervous enough to lose his appetite. He'd gotten the job by answering an ad in the paper. The club owner, B-Kool, had interviewed him over the phone. Now Scooby and Shaggy had to prove they could really be DJ's and spin records. Fred, Daphne, and I had come along as their cheering squad.

We stood alongside the dance floor and watched as kids danced to the music. The walls were hung with framed posters of music stars and there was a stage on the other side of the dance floor. This was the kind of club that only served soda, juice, and water, so teenagers were allowed in. They looked like

SCOOBY-DOO™

and the

DANCE CLUB CURSE

by Suzanne Weyn

SCHOLASTIC INC.

New York   Toronto   London   Auckland   Sydney
Mexico City   New Delhi   Hong Kong   Buenos Aires

ISBN 0-439-58715-8

Designed by Louise Bova

12 11 10 9 8 7 6 5 4 3   3 4 5 6 7 8/0
Printed in the U.S.A.
First printing, November 2003

they were having a terrific time. "Jeepers," I said again. "My radio is broken and I haven't heard any of these new songs. They're great!"

A man in a black-and-red sports suit walked over to us. "Welcome to my club," he said. "I'm the owner, B-Kool. You must be Baggy and Scoob-Doggy-Dogg. I knew because you look like your names. I see you've brought your crew."

"We're the gang, otherwise known as Mystery, Inc., crack detectives," I said. "You can call me V-Dink."

"Detectives, you say? I may need you," B-Kool said.

"Why?" Fred asked.

"I'd rather not get into it right now. But keep your eyes open. You just might see what my problem is before the evening is over. Now let's get this tryout started."

He walked over to the DJ stand, where there were a lot of electronics — speakers, turntables, switches, and dials. "Listen up!" he said into a microphone. The kids gathered close to him. "We have a new pair of DJ's tonight — the electrifying Scoob-Doggy-Dogg and Baggy!"

Scooby and Shaggy joined B-Kool, bowing and waving as the crowd cheered. "Thank you! Thank you!" Shaggy said into the microphone. "My partner and I have chosen songs about our favorite subject — food! I'd like to start with a techno dance remix of the old Alan Sherman favorite, 'On Top of Spaghetti.'"

"Rock and roll!" Scooby barked.

Daphne, Fred, and I looked at one another doubtfully. "'On Top of Spaghetti'?" Fred asked. "Is he kidding?"

I shrugged. Who could ever tell whether Shaggy was being serious? But all around me, kids were dancing. They kept on dancing, too. They really liked the songs. Scooby and Shaggy had spent hours making modern dance mixes of songs like "It's Mashed Potatoe Time," "Found a Peanut," and "The Banana Boat Song."

Shaggy seemed to have an endless list of songs about food and eating. "And

now get down to the sound of 'Eat It,' by Weird Al Yankovic," he announced. The kids cheered and kept dancing.

B-Kool joined us. "Look at those kids. They're wild about Baggy and Scoob-Doggy-Dogg. Those guys definitely have the job," he said. Daphne, Fred, and I grinned and gave Shaggy and Scooby the thumbs up.

The night was just great. Not only did the kids love Scoob and Shaggy, but the kitchen staff kept sending them spare ribs, fries, and sodas. Finally it was time for the club to close for the night. We'd been looking, but so far we hadn't seen any problem at the club. "And now for our final song of the night, 'I Want Candy,' sung by Aaron Carter," Shaggy announced.

I spotted B-Kool on the other side of the dance floor. Judging from his expression, it looked to me like he was pretty worried about something.

The song ended — but the kids didn't

stop dancing. "Thanks, everyone," Shaggy spoke into the microphone. "That's it. It's time to go. You can stop dancing now."

"We can't!" a boy shouted as he spun around.

"My feet won't stop moving!" a girl wailed.

The gang and I exchanged worried glances. Was this the problem B-Kool had talked about earlier? Then, by the back wall of the dance floor, a spinning ball of light grew larger and larger!

CHAPTER 2

The blinding ball of light grew so big that it nearly filled the room. Then the ball of light popped — and standing there was a female rock star. Well . . . sort of.

She wore jeans and a bell-sleeved shirt. Her hair was blond . . . and black . . . and orange. She had a different hair color on each of her three heads! That's right! Three heads bobbed slowly on the end of three long, snake-like necks.

The kids on the dance floor gasped and screamed, but they still couldn't stop dancing. "Yikes!" cried Shaggy. "That's one pop sensation who just popped in from out of nowhere!"

The creature held a microphone and

began to sing into it — if you
could call it singing. It was
more like shrieking. I
covered my ears. "Jinkies,"
I said. "She's awful."

"And who does her
hair?" Daphne asked.
"All three of those heads
need a makeover."

"Behold the greatest
rock diva the world has
ever known," the creature
screeched. "It is I, the one-woman girl
group — Triple Threat! I've put a spell
on this club. None of you will be able to
stop dancing until you listen to me perform all the songs from my new CD,
Three Times the Horror."

She began shrieking a really awful
song. And it didn't seem to have an end-
ing. It just went on and on and on! "Do
something, Shaggy," Daphne pleaded.
"Play a song to drown out Triple Threat's
terrible voice."

Shaggy played "Sugar, Sugar," by the Archies. But Triple Threat just pumped up the volume on her own horrible singing. All three heads shrieked and howled. I couldn't make out a single word they were singing. It all just sounded like screechy, scratchy scream-ing — in three-headed stereo.

The kids were helpless. No matter what they did, they couldn't stop danc-ing. B-Kool joined us. He had to shout so we could hear him over Triple Threat's singing. "Now do you see my problem? Triple Threat started appearing two nights ago. That's why I needed to hire new DJ's. The old ones are so scared, they won't work here anymore."

Triple Threat hit a note so high that the glasses behind the refreshment counter shattered. She kept on singing and singing. Out on the dance floor a girl collapsed from exhaustion and fear. We ran out onto the floor to carry her off. As I passed the dancers I noticed that they all looked a little spacey and dazed. Who could blame them, having to dance to Triple Threat's deafening songs until their muscles ached?

"This is so uncool," B-Kool said as he poured water on the passed-out dancer. Her eyes fluttered open and she seemed to be okay.

"Do you have any idea where that three-headed horror came from?" Fred asked.

B-Kool shook his head. "Not a clue. But speaking of clues, do you kids think you could look around and see if you can find anything?"

"That's what we do best," I replied.

"Sure," Daphne agreed. "No one will suspect us since we're just friends of Shaggy . . . er . . . Baggy and Scoob-Doggy-Dogg."

"Exactly," said B-Kool.

The next morning we went back to DanceKraze to look around. "I'm glad to get out of those baggy pants," Shaggy said. "They kept sliding down and I was tripping over them all night long." He put on one of his dance mixes, a re-make of "Yummy, Yummy (I Have Love in My Tummy)." Shaggy and Scooby went to the middle of the dance floor and began practicing some dance moves. "I can really dance without those pants weighing me down!" Shaggy said.

B-Kool came out and joined Daphne, Fred, and me. "This club was built back in the 1960's," he told us. "Check out this crazy dance floor." He pulled a lever

and the entire floor began spinning slowly in a circle. Then he flipped a switch and a disco ball began turning. The room was lit with swirling specks of colored light.

"Whoa-woa-wo!" Shaggy shouted as his legs kicked up into the air and he fell backward. He hadn't been expecting the dance floor to start moving.

"Rikes!" Scooby yelped. His legs wiggled like rubber bands.

"Sorry, guys," B-Kool said, turning off the floor.

"Like, I think Scoob and I will look for clues in the kitchen," Shaggy said, walking in a dizzy zigzag across the floor. "We'll be safer there."

"Ruch rafer," Scooby agreed as he walked in a circle.

"Gee," said B-Kool. "I set the floor speed on slow. I could have really made it go fast but I didn't. I'm sorry."

"No problem," I said. "Those two are

always happy for an excuse to go to the kitchen. Mind if we look around the club?"

Scooby and Shaggy went to the kitchen while Fred and Daphne checked out the storage rooms behind the dance floor. B-Kool showed me his office upstairs. The walls were lined with pictures of him with lots of different music stars. "How did you meet all these celebrities?" I asked.

"I've worked as a music producer for years," he said. "I recently bought my very own record company. I call it Fizz-Pop Music. Cute, huh? I bought this club to showcase the acts on my record label."

"How's business?" I asked.

"Awesome. Never better," he answered. "Do you think Triple Threat could be the spirit of some disappointed rock star — or maybe an entire rock group — that used to play in this club?"

"Anything's possible, Mr. Kool," I said.

"Please, V-Dink, call me B-Kool," he said. "My real name is Bernard Koolton, but I prefer B-Kool."

"Okay," I agreed. "You can call me Velma."

B-Kool showed me all around the upstairs of the club. He brought me out onto a platform over the dance floor where he sometimes mounted lights for special effects, and showed me a ladder that led to the roof. I didn't find any clues, but it was helpful to see where everything was located. After that, we went down a back staircase to the kitchen. Scooby and Shaggy had built themselves sandwiches that reached the ceiling and were busy trying to fit them into their mouths. "You were supposed to be searching for clues!" I said.

"Mnphmfuftup," was all Shaggy was able to say through a mouth stuffed with sandwich. Scooby just nodded.

"Never mind. Come on," I said as I headed back toward the dance floor.

"I'll be in my office if you need me," B-Kool said, going back up the stairs.

Scooby and Shaggy followed me. We were supposed to meet Fred and Daphne. When we got to the dance floor, they were already standing in the middle of it. We joined them. "Well, Daphne and I didn't find anything that seemed un-usu —" Fred began, then stopped suddenly.

The ball of white light had reappeared. Once again, it grew larger and larger, then popped. Triple Threat was back!

As soon as she started singing, I started dancing — and I couldn't stop! All of us were dancing. My body was moving even though I didn't want it to. I had no control over it! None of us did!

The noise was just as awful as it had been the night before. Triple Threat liked to sing *loudly*, too. She moved around the dance floor, her three heads all off-key. She was moving closer and closer to us.

"I think we'd better get out of here," Scooby said. "But it's hard to run while you're dancing."

"I know," Fred said. "I can't stop."

"I can't, either," Daphne said. "Look, she's almost next to us."

She was right! Triple Threat's three heads stretched toward us. One of its heads was practically nose to nose with me.

Then, from out of nowhere, a huge net swung in our direction. It knocked us off our feet and we fell into it. In the next second, the gang and I were being hoisted high into the air!

CHAPTER 3

We dangled in the air, helpless. What would happen next?

"Hey, peeps. You're safe!" We looked down and saw a boy of about 12. He wore headphones and looked familiar, but I wasn't sure where I'd seen him before. Below us, Triple Threat had stopped shrieking her song. In fact, I couldn't see her anymore. She'd disappeared.

"Yeah, she's gone," the boy said. He had anchored the net to a railing of the platform over the dance floor that B-Kool had shown me. Now he pulled it all the way up to the platform.

"Thanks, pal," Fred said as he untangled himself from the net and climbed out.

"It's lucky you had this net," Daphne said.

"B-Kool had an underwater theme night last week," the boy said. "He strung this net with sparkly electric starfish and hung it over the dance floor. It was awesome. When I saw that the three-headed monster was about to get you, I remembered the net was up here."

"We owe you big time," Shaggy said as he helped Scooby out of the net. He stared at the boy a moment. "Like, I know you," he said. "You're that kid singer, Li'l Donatello!"

"That's me," he said. "I just signed with FizzPop Music and I'm going to perform here tonight. This club was a real dump until B-Kool bought it. Now it's the most happening place in town."

Shaggy and Scooby put their arms around Li'l Donatello. "Like, man, with your singing and our CD-spinning, the place is gonna jump tonight!"

"As long as Triple Threat stays away," Fred reminded them.

Below, B-Kool walked onto the dance

floor. A pretty blond woman stood beside him and they were arguing. "Isn't that Mitzy Monroe, the singer?" Daphne asked.

"Sure is," Li'l Donatello said as he began folding up the net. "She just signed with FizzPop Music, too. She's also singing here tonight."

The gang and I peered down over the platform railing and listened as B-Kool and Mitzy continued to argue. "You may be cool, but you're not being fair!" Mitzy shouted. "When I signed with your music company I was just starting out. Now I'm a big star. I need a big music label behind me. You have to let me out of my contract."

"You signed a three-year contract with me," B-Kool protested. "FizzPop Music helped your career when no one had even heard of you."

"But now everyone's heard of me!" Mitzy cried.

"Mitzy, let's talk about this later," B-Kool said. "I'm closing the club for tonight and I need to phone the staff and tell them not to come in."

"Closing the club?" Li'l Donatello cried. "No way! He can't!" He ran off the platform and headed for the stairs. We followed him down to the dance floor. "B-Kool, you can't do that!" he said when he got to the dance floor. "I'm performing tonight. I've invited the press, important fans, and my mother! Besides, my new CD, *Hungry for Love*, just came out. I need publicity for it."

"Sorry, Donatello. The club has become too dangerous," B-Kool said.

"I'm not afraid of Triple Threat," Li'l Donatello argued. "If she shows up while

I'm singing it will be great publicity. I say bring her on!"

"Not me!" said Mitzy. "I'm not singing if that thing is here!" She turned and stormed out of the club.

B-Kool watched her go and sighed deeply. "That's gratitude for you. When she was just starting, FizzPop Music paid for her clothes, her dancing and singing lessons, her meals — everything! We even paid for a hypnotist to help her stop biting her nails."

"A hypnotist?" Shaggy asked. "You mean, like, a person who suggests that you do something in a way so that you just have to do it?"

"I guess that's the idea," B-Kool said. "I don't know what to do. Maybe I shouldn't close the club tonight."

"I sure hope you don't close it. This is our big night," Shaggy told B-Kool. "Two major stars are performing at the same time Scoob-Dogg and I will be the DJ's."

"*Three* major stars," said a good-looking young guy as he strode confidently into the club. It was Rusty Weel, the singing star.

"Rusty, my man," B-Kool said, slapping palms with the star. "Are you joining Mitzy and Donatello on stage tonight?"

"I think so," he said. "We music execs have to support one another."

"Rusty started a music label of his own, Hoppy Music," B-Kool explained to us. "There are no hard feelings, though. There's room for everyone."

"You said it," Rusty agreed.

"Okay, then," B-Kool said. "Since Rusty came down to perform tonight, I guess I owe it to him to stay open."

"All right!" Shaggy cheered. He and Scooby slapped one another with a high five. Shaggy turned to Rusty. "Allow us to introduce ourselves. We're this town's freshest new DJ's, Baggy and Scoob-Doggy-Dogg."

"Glad to meet you," Rusty said. "If you

don't mind, I'd like to run through some dance moves. Could you spin my latest CD for me so I can practice?"

"Absolutely," Shaggy said. He and Scooby went to the sound system and put on their headphones. They began playing the music. Rusty started dancing, doing the great moves he was known for.

"Why don't we look around for some more clues," Fred suggested.

"You and Daphne go," I said. "I'll be in the Mystery Machine doing some Internet research on my laptop computer. I want to see what I can find out about Li'l Donatello, B-Kool, Mitzy Monroe, and Rusty Weel. They're all suspects. Li'l Donatello wants publicity for his new CD, and B-Kool might want publicity for his club. And Mitzy Monroe sure seemed angry at B-Kool. She might want to hurt the club for some reason."

"Why would you suspect Rusty Weel?" Daphne asked.

"I don't know," I admitted. "But he's here, so I'm going to see what I can learn about him."

CHAPTER 4

I didn't actually see what happened next because I was out in the Mystery Machine working on my computer. But later Shaggy told me what went on.

They were playing Rusty Weel's songs while he practiced his dance moves. Then suddenly the big ball of bright light appeared and Triple Threat popped out of it. She stood on the stage, her heads weaving and bobbing in all directions. At first, Rusty didn't see her. He was too busy spinning on his shoulder. But Scooby and Shaggy saw her. They were glad they had headphones on so they couldn't hear her awful singing.

Triple Threat moved off the stage and crossed the dance floor, coming closer to Rusty. She reached out toward him as she shrieked her song. Her three necks stretched in his direction and her three heads bobbed.

Rusty turned and saw Triple Threat coming at him. He started screaming — but he couldn't stop dancing. And when Rusty danced he *really* danced. He spun and kicked in the air. He turned and flipped. Shaggy could see that he was trying to run away from Triple Threat, but couldn't.

Shaggy and Scooby knew they had to do something to help Rusty. For some reason, the dancing spell wasn't affecting them. Thinking fast, Shaggy and Scooby picked up CD's and tossed them toward Triple Threat like Frisbees. They sliced through the air, hitting the three-headed rock monster.

Being hit with CD's made Triple Threat mad! Her singing became louder and more high-pitched. She started moving away from Rusty and right toward Scooby and Shaggy.

They didn't have to talk about it. Shaggy and Scooby knew what to do. It was what they always did at times like this. They held on to their headphones and ran!

And Triple Threat went after them! She chased them out of their DJ stand, down the hall, through the kitchen, up the stairs, down the stairs, and back toward the dance floor. All the while, her terrible shrieking filled the club.

Scooby and Shaggy raced down the hall ahead of Triple Threat. As they

headed for the dance floor, one of her heads stretched forward until it was right next to Scooby's. He looked to the side and saw it. With a yowl of panic, he jumped into Shaggy's arms. Shaggy wasn't expecting that! With Scooby in his arms, he staggered into the wall by the DJ stand. He bounced off the wall, sending the poster of Cher crashing to the ground.

They didn't stop to pick it up, but just kept going. Finally, they stopped in the middle of the dance floor. "I think that Triple Trouble is gone!" Shaggy said breathlessly. They looked all around and didn't see her. They only saw Rusty sprawled on the floor, where he'd collapsed from exhaustion.

That's when I came back inside. "Guess what I found out!" I said.

Fred and Daphne ran in at the same time. "We found an important clue," Daphne said.

I looked over at a fallen poster. "I think Scooby and Shaggy have found something important, too." I led the others over to look at the smashed poster of Cher on the floor. It had a narrow cabinet built onto the back of it. When the guys knocked the poster down, the cabinet had smashed open. Its contents — a tape recorder and a digital video projector —lay broken on the floor.

"Look," Daphne said, picking up the broken poster. "A hole has been cut into this poster of Cher. Maybe the projector shines the ball of light through this hole every time Triple Threat appears."

Fred took the tape out of the smashed tape recorder. The tape had been pulled out of its case and was all tangled. "It looks like Triple Threat — or someone — destroyed this tape after it fell. It's not marked, either. There's no way to tell what's on it."

"Hmm," Daphne said. "Maybe the

clues we found will shed some light on that." We followed her back to the middle of the dance floor. She and Fred had put a book down there. "We found this book in a cleaning supply cabinet when we were looking  around," she told the rest of us.

I picked up the book and read the title. "*The Secrets of Hypnotism* by Dowhat Isay."

"Velma, you said you found out something," Daphne said. "What was it?"

"I searched a few celebrity gossip websites and found out plenty," I said. "It turns out that Mitzy Monroe and Rusty Weel have been dating." As I was talking,

I noticed something out on the dance floor and went to pick it up. It was a flesh-colored piece of rubber.

Fred took it from me and examined it. "I think I might know what this is," he said. "And I think it's time to put a plan into action."

CHAPTER 5

"Jeepers! I've never seen so many music stars," I said that night. Limousines pulled up outside DanceKraze and all sorts of celebrities piled out of them. The gang and I lined up to get in. Everyone watched as the stars were hurried past the velvet ropes and into the club.

"What did you say?" Fred shouted at me.

"He's already put in his earplugs," Daphne explained. "We're almost at the front of the line, so you and I should put them in, too, Velma." We popped in our earplugs. Scooby and Shaggy would be wearing their DJ headsets, so they wouldn't need the plugs. We'd figured out that since Scooby and Shaggy hadn't been affected by Triple Threat when they'd had on headphones, and Li'l Donatello hadn't been affected when he wore his Walkman, *hearing* must have something to do with Triple Threat's power. If we couldn't hear, then we wouldn't fall under the dancing spell — or at least we hoped it would work that way.

The guard at the front of the line noticed us waiting and waved us in. "Is everything set?" I asked Fred when we were inside the club.

"What?" he shouted.

He took out his plugs. Daphne and I did the same. "Is everything set?" I repeated.

He nodded. "All set to go. Now we just need Scooby and Shaggy to lure out Triple Threat."

"Oh, no!" Shaggy protested, shaking his head. "Not again. Like, Scoob and I are celebrity DJ's now. This crowd expects us to rock the house tonight. We can't be off luring out creepy three-headed monsters."

Daphne reached into her bag and pulled out a box. "Would you do it for a Scooby Snack?"

Scooby and Shaggy shook their heads. "Nothing could make us disappoint our loyal fans," Shaggy said. "There is no way we would let down the music-loving kids who came here counting on us to play music."

"Reah, ro ray." Scooby agreed.

"Would you do it for this whole box of Scooby Snacks?" Daphne asked.

"Okay," Shaggy quickly agreed, snapping the box out of her hands. "Where do you want us to lure her?"

"Off the stage and onto the dance floor," Fred told them. "When Triple Threat appears, I'll find some way to clear the dance floor. Then you and Scooby get out there and do something to make her go after you. Velma and Daphne, you know what to do after that."

"We're on it," I said.

B-Kool hurried up to us. "It's time for Baggy and Scoob-Doggy-Dogg to go on. What are you going to do if Triple Threat shows up?"

"We're ready for her," Shaggy told him. He swallowed nervously. "At least I hope we are." He turned to Scooby. "Come on, Scoob. Our fans are waiting." They put on their headphones and went to the DJ stand.

B-Kool jumped in front of them and spoke into the microphone. "Give it up for Baggy and Scoob-Doggy-Dogg!" he said. The kids on the dance floor started clapping. Shaggy and Scooby pumped their arms in the air and danced around the DJ stand. Then B-Kool lowered the lights and the kids started to dance to Shaggy's techno dance update of "Sugarpie, Honeybunch," by the Four Tops.

As the kids danced, a ball of light started to glow on the stage. Fred didn't waste a moment. Before any of the dancing kids noticed the ball of light, he hurried to the DJ stand and grabbed the microphone. "Li'l Donatello is signing autographs in the front hall," he announced. "The first twenty people there also get a copy of his new CD, *Hungry for Love*." Just as we'd hoped, all the kids rushed off the dance floor toward the front hall to see Li'l Donatello.

Scooby and Shaggy headed that way, too, but Fred stopped them. "You're getting Triple Threat to chase you. Remember?"

"We didn't forget," Shaggy answered. "We were hoping you guys forgot."

"Get going," Daphne said.

The ball of light was getting larger and larger. It popped and Triple Threat appeared. Daphne and I hurried to our places.

Triple Threat began her horrible

singing. Scooby and Shaggy went out onto the dance floor. They began spinning, kicking, and twirling. The three-headed creature began moving closer to them. Her three necks stretched out. "Scoob, I want to run away, but I can't stop dancing!" Shaggy wailed.

That was our cue to act!

Triple Threat lunged toward Scooby and Shaggy. That's when Daphne switched on the colored lights and the disco ball. I pulled a lever that activated the rotating dance floor. I yanked the stick all the way up to HIGH so that the floor was really spinning fast.

Triple Threat was suddenly confused and thrown off balance. Shaggy barely had to touch her. One little poke sent her flying. Her feet shot up in the air as she lost her footing and fell backward. Her three heads flew off in three different directions.

Scooby and Shaggy jumped off the moving dance floor as I pushed the lever

to OFF and Daphne cut the colored spinning lights. Fred flicked on the bright
ceiling lights. "Now let's see who's *really*
under those three shrieking heads," he
said.

CHAPTER 6

A familiar face popped out from under Triple Threat's shirt. "It's Mitzy Monroe!" Fred said.

B-Kool ran up to join us. "Mitzy, how could you do this to me? Why?"

"I told you I didn't want to be part of FizzPop Music anymore," she replied angrily.

Rusty Weel came in. "Mitzy!" he cried. "You're Triple Threat?"

"I'm surprised you didn't know," I said. "Yesterday when I was doing some research on the Internet, I learned that you and Mitzy are dating. She wants to join you at your new music company, Hoppy Music. You've known one another ever since you were on *Puppet Time* together as little kids."

"That's where Mitzy learned to work these three puppet heads," Fred said, holding up Triple Threat's one blond head.

"And she learned about hypnotism when B-Kool sent her to a hypnotist to help her stop biting her nails," I said. "Anything she didn't know, she taught herself from the book Fred and Daphne found yesterday."

"And Triple Threat's dancing spell was really a hypnotic suggestion that was playing on a recorder behind the Cher poster," Daphne added. She held up a tape recorder and pressed the play button.

"You can't stop dancing until Triple Threat stops singing," said a voice that sounded like Mitzy's. "You can't stop dancing until Triple Threat stops singing," the voice repeated over and over.

"You played this tape very softly so

that the kids would be hypnotized by it," I said. "When Triple Threat started singing, they would be hypnotized to think they couldn't stop. Yesterday, Li'l Donatello was able to save us because he had on headphones. He never heard the hypnotic suggestion."

"You grabbed the tape after Scooby and Shaggy knocked it down," Fred went on. "But we found another one in another poster. We changed the tape. That's why Scooby and Shaggy were really able to stop dancing tonight."

"Why did you think I'd release you from your contract just because I had a haunted club?" B-Kool asked.

"I knew FizzPop Music was counting on the club to show off its performers," Mitzy said. "I figured that if the club was haunted, kids would stop coming. If the club failed, then the music label would fail, too. If there was no FizzPop Music company, I'd be free to join Rusty over at Hoppy Music. And I would have gotten away with it, too, if it wasn't for you meddling kids."

"Well, I release you from your contract," B-Kool said. He took her contract from his pocket and ripped it to pieces. "I don't want you on FizzPop."

"I don't want you at Hoppy, either," Rusty said. "Would you try to ruin my business, too, if you were angry at me?"

"It looks like you don't have a record deal at all anymore," B-Kool said.

Mitzy stood up. Her face grew red and she let out a shriek as she stamped her feet angrily.

"She sounds just like Triple Threat," Fred said.

The kids were slowly coming back onto the dance floor with Li'l Donatello. "Let's get this party started!" he shouted as he jumped up onto the stage. "Tonight I'm going to sing from my new CD, *Hungry for Love*," he said. "And I'd like to dedicate my performance to Mystery, Inc."

"I'm going to have to get a new radio so I can listen to all the FizzPop Music singers," I told B-Kool. "I'm sure *Hungry for Love* will be on the radio all the time."

"I'm hungry, but not for love," Shaggy said. "Right now I could go for a pizza with extra everything."

"Come to the kitchen. I'll order whatever you want," B-Kool said with a smile.

"Could we get one with Scooby Snacks on top?" Shaggy asked.

"Extra Scooby Snacks," B-Kool agreed.

Scooby licked his lips. "Rooby-rooby-roo!" he barked.